Flower Girls #2
Daisy

For my sister Debby

Harper Trophy® is a registered trademark of HarperCollins Publishers Inc.

Daisy

Text copyright © 1997 by Kathleen Leverich

Illustrations copyright © 1997 by HarperCollins Publishers Inc.

Library of Congress Cataloging-in-Publication Data

Leverich, Kathleen.

Daisy / by Kathleen Leverich ; illustrated by Lynne Woodcock Cravath.

p.   cm. — (Flower Girls ; #2)

Summary: Daisy must learn to sing in harmony when she and three other girls are chosen to be flower
girls at her grandfather's wedding.

ISBN 0-06-442019-1 (pbk.)

[1. Weddings—Fiction.   2. Singing—Fiction.   3. Grandfathers—Fiction.]   I. Cravath, Lynne
Woodcock, ill.   II. Title.   III. Series: Leverich, Kathleen.   Flower Girls ; #2.

PZ7.L5744Dai   1997   96-8469

[Fic]—dc20   CIP

                                                                                                                                    AC

2   3   4   5   6   7   8   9   10

❖

First Edition

Flower Girls #2

Daisy

by Kathleen Leverich

Illustrated by Lynne Woodcock Cravath

HarperTrophy®
A Division of HarperCollinsPublishers

Chapter 1

Daisy Bliss was headed for trouble.

An alarm bell in her mind told her so.

For a day and a night that bell had been ringing faintly but steadily. All because of the unexpected news.

Trouble was the last thing eight-year-old Daisy usually thought about. She was the prettiest girl in her school and the most popular.

Daisy had dark brown skin, dark brown eyes, and five hundred neat, chin-length black braids.

She could do more chin-ups than anyone in the third grade, boys included.

She could hit a softball farther.

In gym class all the kids wanted Daisy on their team.

At lunch all the kids wanted to sit next to her.

Daisy always felt special.

She always felt envied and admired.

Troubled was a way Daisy never felt. . . .

Or she hadn't until now.

"I hear car horns!" Daisy's friend Violet sat up straight.

Rose and Heather sat up straight, too.

Daisy put the trouble from her mind and turned to watch.

It was the third Sunday in June, and it was hot.

Daisy and her best friends were sitting on their usual bench in Pleasant Park. It was the Flower Girl bench, named for their club: the Flower Girls.

The idea for the club was simple.

Each of the four members had a flower name. Each wanted to be a real flower girl in a wedding.

Every weekend they met in the best place in town to see weddings: this spot.

"I see the first car!" said Rose.

Daisy watched as a car decorated with balloons and crepe-paper streamers pulled up to the edge of the park.

Three bridesmaids in tight-fitting, ankle-length lime-green gowns slid out of the car.

Three ushers dressed in dinner jackets followed them onto the path.

Every couple in town came to Pleasant Park to have their wedding photos taken.

In spring the bridal parties gathered by the pond while ducks swam past. In summer the brides and grooms posed in the Japanese teahouse, where they kissed and kissed and kissed. Gusty winds swirled in autumn while bridesmaids struggled to hold the bride's veil and train in place. In winter the bridal parties rode through the park in horse-drawn sleighs.

Daisy liked summer weddings best. She liked summer everything best.

"There's a second car!" said Violet.

"There's a third!" said Rose.

"There she is!" Heather pointed.

"Where?" Violet looked.

She wasn't the bride. *She* was the girl around their age who was scrambling out of the third car. She wore a short, lace-trimmed, lemon-yellow dress and a

4

straw bonnet trimmed with ivory rib-
bons and yellow rosebuds.

She ran past bridesmaids and ushers
toward the ducks on the grass, scattering
them.

She was the flower girl.

"What do you think?" said Heather.

Rose spoke first. "That flower girl is
pretty, but she acts immature. . . ."

Rose was tall, thin, and delicate-looking. She had long red hair and the palest skin. "A flower girl has to act dignified. She can't shriek and run around."

Some people said Rose was too serious. She was bossy and acted like a grown-up. Daisy said maybe Rose did, but Rose had better ideas than anyone else. Rose was a leader. She always tried to be fair, and she had good judgment. The idea for the Flower Girls club had been hers.

Violet said, "I think that flower girl is acting silly on purpose. She probably feels shy with all the grown-ups."

Violet was quiet and thoughtful. With her chin-length black hair, her big dark eyes, and her crisply ironed dresses, Violet reminded Daisy of a beautiful but easily broken doll.

"I feel shy with grown-ups some-times." Violet said it as if she were telling a deep dark secret.

"You feel shy with your own shadow!" said Heather.

Violet looked embarrassed. Some kids called her "Shrinking Violet" because she was timid and always hung back. "I'd act outgoing if I were a standout like Daisy. But I'm not. So I can't."

Praise always made Daisy feel generous. She jumped up and did a handstand on the grass. "You're special in your own way, Violet. You notice things that other people miss."

Violet looked at her shoes and blushed.

"I notice things too!" Heather folded her arms and tossed her head. "For example, the groom and his ushers are wearing dinner jackets. And it's not even noon!"

At seven and a half, Heather was younger than the other Flower Girls. She was short and sturdy, and she had a cloud of honey-colored hair that she tossed whenever she made a point. Her eyes were honey-colored too.

Some people called Heather a snob because she found something wrong with everyone and everything.

Some people said she had a big mouth because she said exactly what she thought.

Everyone said she had thin skin. The least criticism upset her.

But Heather was funny, and she was smart. Smart enough to have skipped first grade. Heather was an excellent friend as long as you knew how to handle her.

Daisy knew how. Handling difficult people was what Daisy did best. She turned a somersault. "When I plan my wedding, I'll consult you, Heather."

Heather sniffed and tossed her head, but Daisy could tell she was pleased.

Rose joined Daisy on the grass. "Only three weeks until that flower girl will be you!"

Daisy followed Rose's gaze across the pond to the spot where the pretty but immature and possibly shy flower girl stood. She imagined herself standing in that spot. . . .

It gave her a summery feeling all over. "I never expected to be a flower girl for my grandaddy!"

Daisy's grandaddy Lester was the librarian at the local college. He had been a widower since before Daisy was born. Now he was going to remarry. His fiancée, Dr. Adele Legerdemain, was a chemistry professor and a widow. She had arrived at the college just six months earlier. When people asked Grandaddy Lester to explain their lightning-fast romance, he would grin and say, "That woman put a spell on me!"

The wedding would be on July 11 at the Good News Baptist Church. The reception would be at the college's faculty club. Photographs would be taken here in Pleasant Park. Dr. Adele had asked Daisy to be her flower girl.

"Daisy will be the best flower girl ever!" Heather's voice was envious.

"Daisy's best at everything she does." Rose was matter-of-fact.

 10

Violet sighed. "No one's as special as Daisy."

"Cut it out, you guys!" Daisy rolled her eyes as if her friends' admiration embarrassed her.

The truth was, Daisy loved admiration. Ever since she'd been a little girl, people had been telling her she was "the best." At first she'd been pleasantly startled. Then she'd gotten used to it. Now she had to be "the best" at everything she did. If Daisy wasn't the best, who was she?

"Daisy will be the star of her grandad's wedding!" Violet sat on the grass. Her crisply ironed dress spread around her.

Heather hopscotched over an imaginary grid on the grass. She stopped to grin. "Everyone but Daisy will have wrinkles and gray hair!"

The alarm bell in Daisy's mind clanged.

"Everyone but Daisy will be old and crotchety!" Rose giggled as she collapsed on her back.

Now's the time to tell the news, thought Daisy. She tried to sound matter-of-fact. "Everyone but the other flower girls."

Heather's grin dimmed.

Violet looked puzzled. "There will be others . . . ?"

"Three others." Daisy shrugged off the news as if it were nothing. "Dr. Adele's granddaughters."

"We never heard about any granddaughters." Rose sat up.

Those granddaughters had been a surprise to Daisy, too. Dr. Adele hadn't mentioned them until yesterday. The moment she had . . . the moment Daisy realized she would be one of four flower girls instead of the only one . . . the alarm bell had started to ring.

"Dr. Adele says her granddaughters are 'charmers.' She says they 'enchant' everyone they meet." Daisy was more bothered than she wanted to let on.

Violet smiled encouragingly. "All grandmothers brag, Daisy."

"It's a grandmother law," said Heather. "They have to!"

Rose fell back on the grass and grinned at the sky. "Even if a kid is totally dopey, her grandmother says she's special!"

Daisy felt better. The alarm bell in her mind didn't stop clanging, but it quieted down.

Chapter 2

A week and a half later Daisy and her friends were on their way to swim at Slow Creek. They wore their bathing suits. They had their towels wrapped around their waists. They were walking down the road when an old but gleaming black sedan rumbled past them. It had running boards and rounded contours. It was the kind of oversize automobile that people in old-fashioned mystery movies drove.

Heather pointed. "That's Dr. Adele's car!"

Daisy watched the sedan brake to a stop.

A woman with salt-and-pepper hair leaned out the driver's window. "Hop in, you girls!" she called to them. "I'll give you a lift."

Daisy and her friends ran to the car.

Rose, Violet, and Heather scrambled into the backseat.

Daisy climbed into the front.

Dr. Adele had curly hair, which her stylist cut close to her head. Her skin was the same dark brown as Daisy's. *Mahogany,* she called it. Dr. Adele came from the tropics, and she talked with a singsong accent Daisy loved to hear.

"Fasten your seat belts, children! We are off."

Dr. Adele was dressed in an electric-blue silk suit.

Dr. Adele always wore a straight-skirted, short-jacketed suit. She owned that same suit in dozens of colors.

Dr. Adele also wore chunky gold

earrings, wine-colored lipstick, and wine-colored nail polish. The briefcase by her side was so highly polished, Daisy could see her reflection in the burgundy leather.

Daisy smiled at the reflection.

The best girl in the world smiled back.

Dr. Adele looked at Daisy with amusement. It was as if she could read Daisy's mind . . . the selfish thoughts as well as the good ones.

Daisy hurried to cover up. "We've been talking about your granddaughters. We can't wait to meet them. Will they be here soon?"

Dr. Adele smiled. "My granddaughters arrive from the island in an hour. I'm on my way to the airport to pick them up."

Rose leaned forward. "Which island?

A tropical island? I've never been to an island in the tropics. Is it nice?"

Daisy blinked. She hadn't given a thought to where Dr. Adele's granddaughters might be from. She hadn't given a thought to anything about them. All she'd wondered was, *What will they think of* me?

"Paradise is what the island is!" Dr. Adele peered at Rose in the rearview mirror. "And the islanders are the finest people you'll ever meet."

There she goes, thought Daisy, *bragging again.*

Dr. Adele went on. "My granddaughters won't know a single child here. I'm counting on you girls to make them feel at home."

"If they're athletic like Daisy, we can

take them swimming or bike riding or bowling," said Rose.

"We can give a party for them. We can introduce them to lots of kids," said Heather.

Violet said, "They can play Princess with the dress-up clothes in my mother's trunk."

"What about you, Daisy? You must have an idea," said Dr. Adele.

"An idea?" Daisy couldn't have cared less, but she wanted Dr. Adele to think she was considerate. Generous. The best. She put on an earnest expression. "What would they enjoy? What do your granddaughters like to do?"

Dr. Adele gave Daisy a sidelong glance.

Daisy had the feeling she was reading her mind again.

"My granddaughters like to sing."

"Sing?" said Daisy.

Heather nudged Daisy from behind. She rolled her eyes and mouthed one word, *Bor-ring!*

"They sing close harmonies. In three parts." Dr. Adele swung the wheel to make a left turn. "I hope you sing."

Daisy sang all the time. She was in the school chorus. At most chorus performances, Daisy got to stand up front and sing a solo. Not that she had the best voice. Daisy's voice was just average. She got picked to be soloist because she was Daisy. She was as popular with the music teacher as she was with everyone else.

Daisy shrugged. "I like to sing just fine."

"Good!" said Dr. Adele. "I guarantee that my granddaughters will cook up a musical number for you flower girls to perform at the wedding."

Daisy imagined herself standing by the church altar. She'd be wearing a long, lacy dress. Dr. Adele and Grandaddy Lester would stand to one side of her in their wedding clothes. Dr. Adele's three granddaughters would stand behind her.

Daisy would take a deep breath, open her mouth, and sing. Solo. All the congregation would gaze at her in admiration. Following Daisy's solo, Dr. Adele's granddaughters would join in with harmonies. No one would notice them. Every eye would stay fixed on Daisy. . . .

"Slow Creek Beach, everyone out!" Dr. Adele braked to a stop.

21

Heather, Violet, and Rose scrambled out of the backseat and ran for the creek. "Thanks, Dr. Adele!"

Dr. Adele planted a kiss on Daisy's cheek. "Come to my house bright and early tomorrow. You can meet my granddaughters. The four of you can make plans."

Daisy climbed out of the car and shut the door. "Fine."

Dr. Adele stepped on the gas. Her big black car pulled away.

Daisy waved until it rounded a bend and disappeared. Then she kicked off her sandals and waded into the water ahead of her friends.

Heather snorted. "Singers! Dr. Adele's granddaughters sound like total zeros. I just hope they don't embarrass you too much at the wedding."

"Cut it out, Heather." Rose's nose and shoulders were white with globs of sunblock. She started to rub it into her skin. "We should feel sorry for those girls and be nice to them."

Violet edged sideways into the creek. "Maybe they're more interesting than they sound."

"No way!" Heather flung herself into the water and thrashed toward the float.

Daisy was glad her friends weren't impressed by Dr. Adele's unknown granddaughters.

She eased into the water. "I'm sure they sing well."

She didn't mean what she said. But as the best, most popular girl in town she could afford to be kind.

Daisy leaned back into the water. She stretched out her arms, closed her eyes, and floated.

Chapter 3

Daisy awakened the next day to the sight of storm clouds massed outside her bedroom window.

Lightning forked the darkened sky while she dressed.

Thunder rumbled overhead while she ate her breakfast.

Daisy climbed into her mother's car. On the way to Dr. Adele's house the streets were so dark the streetlights shone. A storm seemed ready to break, but no rain fell.

Daisy's mother pulled into Dr. Adele's driveway.

Daisy scanned the wrap-around front porch.

There in the porch swing sat Dr. Adele.

Perched like birds on the railing beside her sat three girls.

Daisy slid out of the car.

She walked with her mother to the house. She climbed the porch steps. All the while she sized up those girls.

The oldest girl looked about eleven years old. Daisy guessed the youngest was seven. The middle girl hopped off the railing. She caught Daisy's eye, raised a hand, and folded down her fingers one by one. The corners of her mouth lifted in a slow grin.

She's my age, thought Daisy.

Then she thought, *But I look more grown-up. . . .*

All three had coffee-colored skin. The eldest was dark coffee. The youngest, coffee with lots of cream. The middle, coffee with a splash of milk and a sprinkle of cinnamon.

Each girl's curly hair was cut close to her head. Gold earrings dangled from each girl's earlobes. The oldest girl's earrings were fiery-rayed suns. The youngest's were tiny stars. Crescent moons dangled from the middle girl's ears.

Those moons, suns, and stars shone in the gloomy morning as brightly as . . .

The real things! thought Daisy.

"Don't stare, sweetheart," whispered Daisy's mother.

Daisy shook herself. Those twirling earrings had put her into a trance.

She climbed the porch steps.

Dr. Adele came forward to meet them. She gestured to the girls on the railing. "My eldest granddaughter, Glory. My youngest, Jade . . ."

The girls nodded to Daisy as Dr. Adele introduced them.

Each wore a gauzy dress in a pearly shade. Glory's was ivory. Jade's, amber.

"Persia is my in-between."

Persia's dress was the palest amethyst.

Daisy ran her eyes over the three girls and thought, *Those girls don't look as athletic as I am. They don't seem like most-popular-girl-in-school types. They're pretty, but nothing special. . . .*

Daisy let that thought trail off.

Something about those girls' looks *was* special. . . .

 28

Daisy realized then. It was their unusual eyes.

Glory's were ice-blue.

Jade's, sea-green.

The silver of Persia's eyes reminded Daisy of rain.

Dr. Adele opened the screen door. "Daisy's mother and I are going inside for a chat. You girls stay out here and get acquainted."

The porch door swung shut behind them.

Daisy and the girls were alone on the porch.

Jade swung her legs against the railing. "People call us 'the granddaughters.'"

Glory smiled. "Once your grandad marries Gran Adele, you'll be a 'granddaughter' too."

No way! thought Daisy.

She smiled as if Glory had said something kind but incorrect. "You're granddaughters. I'll be a *step*granddaughter. I'll always be a little different from you."

Glory raised an eyebrow.

Persia and Jade exchanged a look.

I guess I made my point, thought Daisy.

She crossed the porch to the fan-back wicker chair that looked like a throne.

She sat in it and felt secure and in charge. She put on her friendliest expression. "Your grandmother brags all the time about you! You must be awfully special."

Daisy waited for them to say, *Gran Adele brags to us about you! She tells us you're the best, most popular girl in town. . . . Hey, you should sing a solo with us . . . !*

"Gran Adele brags?" said Persia.

"She hasn't told us a thing about you," said Jade.

Glory met Daisy's eye. "What exactly did Gran Adele say?"

The question took Daisy by surprise. She tried to remember what Dr. Adele had said to Rose the day before.

"Dr. Adele said . . . she said you come from an island." Daisy congratulated herself on remembering. She relaxed into the chair.

Glory nodded. "That's true, but it's not bragging. What else?"

What else? thought Daisy.

She felt hot and sticky.

"Well?" said Glory.

Thunder boomed in the distance.

"Dr. Adele calls you charmers. She says you enchant people." The words flowed out of Daisy's mouth before she could stop them. She thought a minute, then added, "You haven't enchanted me."

Lightning flashed across the sky.

Glory looked at Persia and Jade. She raised an eyebrow. "Should we enchant her?"

Jade gave Daisy a critical look. "She *will* be our stepcousin. . . ."

Persia frowned. "I don't know. Enchantment's not for everyone. . . ."

They started to giggle.

Daisy felt awkward and left out.

This wasn't the way things were supposed to go!

Chapter 4

A few raindrops spattered the front walk.

Daisy tried another tack. "Dr. Adele says you love to sing. She says you sing harmonies. . . ."

Daisy might have said a magic word.

"Harmonies?" The granddaughters looked at her wide-eyed as the sky opened up.

Rain hammered the front walk.

Steam rose from the lawn.

The granddaughters regarded Daisy with new interest.

Glory leaned toward her. "Do *you* sing harmonies?"

Jade squirmed with excitement. "We didn't dare hope!"

"Sing with us at the wedding!" Persia looked eager.

Daisy did her best to appear flustered at all the attention. "I'll sing if you want. But I don't harmonize. I've always been a soloist."

Persia stared. "You'd rather solo than harmonize?"

Daisy ignored the question. "Do you sing with a piano or with an organ?"

"We sing a cappella," said Glory.

"That means unaccompanied," said Jade.

Daisy frowned. "A piano helps any song. I always have one when I solo."

Glory leaned against the porch railing. She shrugged. "Our songs don't have solos."

Persia lounged in the swing seat. "We blend our voices to make one sound."

"One that's deeper and wider than any we could make alone." Jade sat on the top step.

Glory leaned toward Daisy. "One that's enchanting."

Daisy glanced from one to another. Were these girls kidding her? They looked sincere. . . .

She folded her arms. "I don't get it. Sing something now and let me hear."

Glory, Persia, and Jade slid from the railing and gathered in a circle.

Glory sang a note and held it. "Swi-nnng . . ."

Persia sang a higher one and held it. "Swi-nnng . . ."

"Swi-nnng . . ." Jade sang and held a note that was higher still.

Their voices made the air around Daisy shimmer and vibrate. They made Daisy's insides shimmer and vibrate too.

Glory nodded sharply.

The girls sang, " 'Swing low, sweet cha-ri-o-ot . . .' "

Each girl sang the same words, but each pitched her voice to different notes.

As their voices rose and fell, things inside Daisy rose and fell too.

The granddaughters bent together.

The tiny suns, moons, and stars twirled below their ears.

Their voices swelled and blended. "'Coming for to carry me . . .'"

Pleasure swelled in Daisy's chest. She felt as if there were no gravity. As if something larger than she was had emptied her out and filled her up. . . .

She thought, *If the granddaughters' singing feels this good to me, how must it feel to them?*

The granddaughters sang the final note. "'Ho-mmme . . .'"

They drew in their breaths.

Except for the creaking of the swing and the rain's now gentle patter, the porch was silent.

Daisy sank back into the fan-back chair. She hadn't realized she'd been gripping the arms.

"How did you like it?" Glory grinned at her.

"Do you still say we need pianos and solos?" Persia grinned too.

Jade cocked her head. "Now will you sing with us?"

Daisy looked at the granddaughters.

She wanted to join their group. She wanted to have that emptied out and filled up feeling again. But . . . she was a soloist! She had to be soloist! "I'm not sure. Let me hear another song."

Daisy's mother stepped out onto the porch. "No songs now, Daisy. It's time to go."

"But Mom, I need to hear just one more. . . ." Daisy caught sight of Dr. Adele. She let her voice trail off.

Dr. Adele smiled as if she understood Daisy's predicament and enjoyed it. "I knew you'd like my granddaughters' singing. I knew you'd join their group. Tell me, what part will you sing?"

Daisy didn't like being laughed at. She backed up a step. "I sing solos. I don't do harmonies."

Dr. Adele raised an eyebrow. She turned from Daisy to her granddaughters.

"Daisy can sing by herself. No hard feelings," said Glory.

"She can join us if she changes her mind," said Persia.

Jade nodded. "We'll be here tomorrow afternoon, rehearsing."

"Let's go, Daisy!"

Daisy looked. Her mother had already reached the car. "In a second!" She turned back to the others.

Dr. Adele's arms rested on the granddaughters' shoulders. She was smiling down at them. The granddaughters were looking up at Dr. Adele and smiling back.

It was as if they had forgotten all about Daisy.

For the second time that day Daisy felt left out.

Chapter 5

That night Daisy phoned Rose. "Dr. Adele's granddaughters want me to sing with them at the wedding. They begged. They're rehearsing tomorrow at Dr. Adele's house. Want to come listen and help me decide?"

"Of course!" said Rose.

Daisy said, "Let's ask Heather and Violet."

Rose said, "I'll call them. 'Bye."

Daisy hung up the phone. She turned to her cat, Princess.

"Tomorrow Rose, Heather, and Violet will tell the granddaughters just how special I am. Once those clueless girls understand, they'll give me a solo in their song."

"Bedtime, Daisy!" Daisy's mother called from downstairs.

Daisy went into the bathroom to brush her teeth.

Princess followed.

Daisy stood at the sink and grinned at

her reflection in the medicine cabinet mirror.

She leaned toward the mirror the way the granddaughters leaned toward one another when they sang.

"'Swing low, sweet cha-ri-o-ot . . .'"

Princess watched from the toilet seat.

Daisy brushed her teeth. She gargled. She spat. She looked at her reflection and grinned.

She couldn't wait for the next day.

The following afternoon Daisy and her friends reached Dr. Adele's house.

The granddaughters were sitting on the porch railing.

Their gauzy dresses wafted on the breeze. The tiny suns, moons, and stars twirled below their ears.

"Those girls look nice!" whispered Violet.

Daisy didn't answer. She was tired of thinking about the granddaughters. It was time for people to think and talk about her.

She introduced everyone. Then she retreated to the fan-back chair to wait and watch.

Right away Glory drew Rose aside. "You seem older than the others, more mature. . . ."

Rose looked startled but pleased.

Daisy saw Persia sit close beside Violet on the porch's top step. "You remind me *so* much of my best friend back on the island. . . ."

Violet blushed. "I do?"

Jade faced Heather in the porch

swing. "You're younger than your friends. I'll bet you skipped a grade. You must be really smart!"

Heather beamed.

Daisy watched them all from the fan-back chair.

No one paid any attention to her. No one told her she was special . . . "the best."

She sprang to her feet. "If we're going to sing at the wedding, we need to rehearse."

"You're going to sing with us?" asked Glory.

"I will if you give me a solo." Daisy grinned.

Glory sighed. "There are no solos."

"We thought you understood," said Persia.

Daisy glanced at her friends.

Rose looked embarrassed for her.

Heather and Violet looked embarrassed too.

Daisy felt a little uneasy. But she was sure the granddaughters were bluffing. "I'll sing separately then. You go first."

Glory smiled the way Dr. Adele sometimes did. Pityingly. "No, you first," she said. "Really."

Daisy didn't mind singing first. She liked being the center of attention. She took a deep breath, clasped her hands, and began.

"Dai-sy, Dai-sy, give me your
    answer true.
I'm half crazy, all for the love of
    yooouuu. . . ."

Rose, Violet, and Heather swayed in time to the music.

The granddaughters didn't sway, but they paid attention.

Daisy reached the song's final bars.

"But you'll look sweet upon the seat
Of a bicycle built for twooo."

She stopped.

Rose, Violet, and Heather cried, "Yay, Daisy!"

Daisy went back to her chair. She smiled at the granddaughters. "Your turn."

Persia got up from the step.

Jade left the swing.

Glory stood with them in a circle.

Just as the day before, each grand-daughter sang her note and held it.

The air around Daisy shimmered and vibrated. Daisy's insides shimmered and vibrated too.

" 'Swi-ing low, sweet cha-ri-o-ot . . .' "
The granddaughters bent together as they
sang. Their eyes met. Their voices blended.

Pleasure swelled in Daisy's chest.
Again she felt as if there were no gravity.
As if something larger than she was had
emptied her out and filled her up. She
felt as if she would burst. . . .

The granddaughters sang their final
note: " 'Ho-mmme.' "

They drew in their breaths.

For a minute no one said anything.

Heather broke the silence. "Daisy
better sing first at the wedding! If she
sings after you, she'll flop."

Daisy waited for Rose and Violet to
stand up for her.

Rose sucked in her lower lip. She
didn't say anything.

Violet stared at her shoes. She didn't say anything either.

"It's hard to make a solo sound as interesting as harmonies," said Glory.

"Especially harmonies like yours!" said Rose.

Violet nodded hard. "They're the best!"

Daisy stared at her friends. *The best?* Her worst nightmare was coming true.

 50

Chapter 6

The following afternoon was hot and sticky.

Daisy didn't notice. She felt calm again. She felt special and in charge again.

Daisy had a plan.

She lifted the kitchen phone and dialed a number. She waited for someone at Dr. Adele's house to answer.

Princess leaped to the counter.

Daisy reached out her free hand to stroke her. As she stroked she told Princess the plan. "I'm going to join the granddaughters' group. I'll sing whatever part they give me. But I'll sing my part a million times better than they sing theirs."

Princess looked up at her. "Mewww?"

"I'll sing louder and with more feeling than all three granddaughters put together! I won't blend in. I'll stand out! I'll be the best. . . ."

"Hello?" Glory answered the phone.

Daisy made her voice friendly. "I've changed my mind. I want to sing with you. What time is the rehearsal?"

"We can't rehearse," said Glory.

"Relatives invited us to visit," shouted Persia. She must have been standing near Glory.

Jade must have been too. She shouted, "Why don't you come with us?"

Daisy stopped stroking Princess. "Relatives? Your relatives?"

"They'll be yours, too, after the wed-ding," Glory pointed out.

Daisy frowned.

Those relatives wouldn't know her. They'd know Glory, Persia, and Jade. They'd make a big fuss over them. They'd treat Daisy politely, but she wouldn't be the favorite. She'd be just another guest.

"I think I'll stay home," said Daisy.

"Come with us! We can rehearse in the car," said Persia.

Daisy didn't want to. "I'll rehearse with you tomorrow."

"We're going visiting tomorrow, too," said Jade.

Daisy had an idea. "Stop by and teach me my part. I'll practice while you go visiting. When it's time for the wedding rehearsal on Friday, I'll be ready."

"I guess we could," said Glory.

"Great!" Daisy hung up. She turned to Princess. "I'll have time to make my part lots better than theirs. By the time they hear, it will be too late to object!"

Daisy met the granddaughters on her front porch. She waved to Dr. Adele, who waited in the car. Then she turned back to Glory, Persia, and Jade. She spread her arms. "Whatever part you give me I'll sing."

Glory watched Princess make figure eights around Daisy's legs. She said, "Daisy's voice is higher than mine."

Jade cocked her head. "It's lower than Persia's and mine."

"Daisy's voice is just right for rhythm," said Persia.

"Is rhythm important?" said Daisy.

Glory looked startled. "Rhythm is the backbone of the song!"

Jade nodded.

Persia cleared her throat. "It goes like this . . .

"Swinnnggg,
Swinnnggg,
Swinnnggg,
Swinnnggg,
Swinnnggg, chaaa-ri-ottt . . ."

Daisy looked from one grand-daughter to the next. "That's it?"

Jade knelt to stroke Princess. "It sounds dull when you sing it alone, but—"

"I'd like a better part," said Daisy.

"There isn't any. In harmonies each

part is equal," said Glory.

Daisy folded her arms. She looked Glory straight in the eye. "Melody is the best part. Everyone knows that."

Jade let Princess lick her hand. "Even melody sounds dull without the other parts."

"You discovered that when you sang solo." Glory rocked on her toes.

Daisy frowned. She couldn't argue with that.

"Is Daisy giving you trouble?" called Dr. Adele from the big black sedan. She smiled as if she were teasing.

But her voice sounds like a warning, thought Daisy.

She remembered her plan. "I'll sing your rhythm part. I'll work on it from now until the wedding rehearsal. I'll be ready Friday evening. You go visiting and have fun."

Daisy watched Dr. Adele and the granddaughters drive off in the big black sedan. Then she sat on the porch steps and set to work on her part.

As the morning passed, Daisy made a change here, to make the part better. She made an improvement there, to make sure her voice would stand out.

She was practicing the new, improved part when Rose, Violet, and Heather came up the front walk.

"What's that you're singing?" said Rose.

"I'm going to harmonize," said Daisy. "Dr. Adele's granddaughters gave me the rhythm part. It's the song's backbone."

She sang the part with her improvements.

Violet looked puzzled. "That sounds too fancy for a rhythm part."

Violet knew about music. She took piano lessons. "A rhythm part should go more like . . .

"Swinnnggg,
Swinnnggg,
Swinnnggg,
Swinnnggg,
Swinnnggg, chaaa-ri-ottt . . ."

"I know how it should go," said Daisy. "I've improved it a little. I've livened it up."

Rose and Violet looked at one another.

Heather rolled her eyes. "Daiiisyyy . . ."

"I know what I'm doing!" Daisy bristled.

Her friends acted as if she were doing something wrong. But those granddaughters started it. . . !

Daisy said, "I'll be the best singer. You'll see."

Chapter 7

On Friday evening Daisy pedaled her bike to the wedding rehearsal. Her parents had gone early to help set up the rehearsal supper.

Daisy paused at the top of Sentinel Hill. She gazed at the scene below.

The breeze felt like velvet against Daisy's skin. The setting sun turned everything gold.

At the foot of the hill Good News Baptist Church gleamed.

Long shadows lay across the church lawn. Picnic tables set up for the rehearsal supper glimmered in patches of light. So did grown-ups laying out the supper dishes.

Enchanted was how the scene looked to Daisy.

Thrilled was how she felt.

She released her brake and plunged down the hill.

Once the singing started she'd be the most enchanting of all. . . .

Daisy slid off her bike and parked it.

"There you are!" Jade stepped from the church.

"We thought you'd never come!" Persia stepped out too.

Glory followed them. "We can't wait to hear how we'll sound with your part!"

Daisy looked at them smiling down at her from the steps.

Their dresses wafted on the breeze.

Their earrings twirled and glittered.

Their eyes shone.

Daisy wanted to run up the steps to join them.

She wanted to be one of the group.

"Come on!" called Persia.

Daisy stopped herself.

I can't do that! she thought.

She had to show everyone, once and for all, that she was different from the granddaughters . . . better . . . the best!

The rehearsal began smoothly.

The bridesmaids marched down the aisle. Daisy and the three granddaughters followed. Last came Dr. Adele.

Grandaddy Lester met her at the altar rail. They turned to face the minister and practiced saying their vows.

"Ready?" Glory looked from Persia and Jade to Daisy.

The people in the pews leaned forward.

Each granddaughter sang her opening note and held it.

Daisy sang and held her note too.

"'Swing low, sweet cha-ri-o-ott . . .'" sang Glory, Persia, and Jade.

Their voices swelled and blended.

Daisy sang too. But far from blending, Daisy did all she could to make her voice stand out. "'Swi-i-ing lo-o-ow . . .'"

The granddaughters bent together. Their eyes met Daisy's and invited her to join them.

Daisy stepped away. She planted her feet, tipped back her head, and sang as loudly and as distinctively as she could. She added trills to her part. She added falsetto notes. She changed the beat.

" 'Coming for to carry me ho-mmme.' "

The song ended.

Daisy turned to see how the audience had liked it.

Some people stared at her.

Others, including her parents, frowned.

A few commented to one another.

"The harmonies were lovely . . . except for Daisy's part," said one.

"What was that child doing?" said another.

A third shrugged. "She acted as if she were singing a solo."

Daisy flushed with shame.

She stole a glance at Grandaddy Lester and Dr. Adele.

Grandaddy was busy talking to the minister, but Dr. Adele returned her glance.

Dr. Adele smiled as if she felt sorry for Daisy. She shook her head.

Daisy felt embarrassed. Then she felt guilty, then angry at Dr. Adele for making her feel that way.

"We haven't got it yet. Let's try again." Glory acted as if she were speaking to all the girls, but she looked straight at Daisy.

For the second run-through Daisy tried a different approach. Instead of rhythm, she sang melody. When the granddaughters bent together, Daisy bent with them. When they met her eyes and smiled, she smiled back. Daisy acted as if the granddaughters were good friends of hers instead of bitter rivals.

But when their voices swelled and blended, Daisy again made her voice stand out.

The song ended.

Daisy turned to the audience.

The frowns were deeper than before.

The comments were more impatient.

"There was a hole where the rhythm part should have been," said several people.

"Daisy will get it right." Daisy heard her parents reassure those people. "She's just nervous because the granddaughters are such *fine* singers . . . !"

Daisy turned back to the grand-daughters.

"Practice won't help," Glory was saying. "Our singing is as good as it's going to get."

The minister looked from Glory to Daisy and back to Glory. He nodded sympathetically. "We'll see everyone here tomorrow at four o'clock."

People stood. They gathered their things to go home.

Daisy looked at the granddaughters. She had ruined their song at the rehearsal. For all they knew, she would ruin it tomorrow at the wedding. "I guess you'd rather I didn't sing with you," she said.

Glory looked startled. "Why do you say that?"

Persia looked startled too. "You're a flower girl. You're going to be a 'grand-daughter'—"

"Stepgranddaughter," Jade corrected her.

Persia went on, "We wish you sang better, but you're part of the group."

Glory put an arm around Daisy's shoulders. She drew her aside. "You can sing that way tomorrow. But you'll ruin the song, and the wedding guests won't like it."

Daisy frowned. "But—"

Glory held up a hand for silence. "Or you can blend your voice. The song will work, but you won't stand out."

Glory shrugged. "It's your choice."

"Come along, girls," called Dr. Adele from the church doorway.

Daisy followed the granddaughters outside.

She watched them run across the darkened lawn to Dr. Adele's car. The three of them shoved and shrieked as they scrambled into the car.

"Let's go, Daisy!" called her father. He was at the other end of the parking lot lifting her bike onto the car rack.

Daisy took one last look at the grand-daughters. None was what Daisy would call a standout. But together . . .

She watched Dr. Adele's car pull out

and drive away. Through the back window she glimpsed the granddaughters.

Their heads were together. They were giggling.

"Daisy!" called her mother.

Daisy didn't want to blend in. But just for a second she yearned to be part of that homeward-bound, giggling group.

Chapter 8

That night Daisy slept badly.

She tossed.

She turned.

She dreamed she sang a solo and people started to boo. *"One voice isn't as interesting as three! Let's hear the granddaughters. . . ."*

She dreamed she sang the rhythm part exactly the way she was supposed to. She blended her voice. People applauded, but they were applauding the whole group, not Daisy. . . .

Daisy awakened with a start.

Sunlight streamed into her bedroom.

Her mother was shaking her gently by the shoulder. "Rise and shine, Daisy! Were you dreaming? You moaned in your sleep."

"That wasn't moaning. It was singing." Daisy rubbed her eyes and shuddered. "I wasn't having a dream. It was a nightmare."

Daisy's mother laid out Daisy's freshly pressed flower girl dress. "The bride and groom are supposed to be the ones with wedding day nerves, not the flower girl. Just sing your part the way the grand-daughters taught it to you. Sing your best, and we'll be proud of you."

Daisy sat up in bed. "I don't want to be a flower girl. I don't want to be in the wedding."

"Hurry and shower. Grace from the

salon is waiting downstairs to do your braids. Once you're dressed you'll feel just fine." Daisy's mother vanished out the door.

Daisy looked at the ribbon-bedecked, pearly yellow dress.

She thought, *I can sing to stand out and get booed. . . .*

She looked at the straw basket full of yellow and white rose petals.

She thought, *I can sing to blend in, but then the granddaughters get all the credit. . . .*

"Daisy, I want to hear that shower water running!" called Daisy's mother.

Daisy sighed.

No matter what she did, she'd run into trouble.

She sighed once more and climbed out of bed.

All the way to the church Daisy argued with herself. She argued with herself as she lined up with the granddaughters in the church vestibule. As the organ sounded the opening chords of the wedding march. As she marched down the aisle scattering yellow and white rose petals.

Jade skipped ahead of her.

Persia marched beside her.

Behind them all came Glory.

They reached the altar rail, moved to the left, and turned to watch.

Grandaddy Lester in his pearl-gray suit stepped to the altar rail.

The bridesmaids filed past him.

Daisy caught sight of Dr. Adele. She wore an ivory silk suit and an expression that said *Lester, I love you.*

She reached the altar rail.

A smile spread over Grandaddy Lester's face. He extended his hand to Dr. Adele.

Together they turned to face the minister.

The service began.

Daisy watched with the granddaughters. She was happy for her grandfather and Dr. Adele. She almost forgot about the song.

Grandaddy Lester and Dr. Adele made their vows.

Glory whispered, "It's time."

Jade and Persia moved closer to form a semicircle.

Daisy didn't know what to do.

Glory sang her note and held it.

Persia sang hers and held it.

Daisy scanned the granddaughters' unworried faces. They didn't think of her as a rival. They didn't think of her as competition. They were going to sing their parts and trust her . . . not to *be* the best, but to *sing* her best.

Glory gave a sharp nod.

Daisy sang the rhythm part. She sang it without trills, without falsetto notes, and without changing the beat. She blended her voice with the others'. She did the best she could.

She and the granddaughters bent together.

Daisy felt the air around her shimmer and vibrate.

They looked into one another's eyes and smiled.

Her insides shimmered and vibrated

too. Pleasure swelled in her chest. She felt as if there were no gravity. As if something larger than she was had emptied her out and filled her up . . .

" 'Coming for to carry me home . . .' " Daisy, Glory, Persia, and Jade sang on. Daisy felt a barrier between them dissolve.

"They're *enchanting*, each and every one of them!" said a guest.

"Even Daisy!" said another.

"A charmer is what that child is!" said a third.

Daisy felt better than charming. She felt better than enchanting. Daisy felt untroubled. Unworried. Content.

Chapter 9

After the ceremony the bridal party drove to Pleasant Park.

The photographer posed Dr. Adele and Grandaddy Lester in the Japanese tea-house.

Click!

She said, "Bridesmaids, ushers, everyone else, I'd like you under the willow trees."

Click!

She said, "Let's have a shot over by the pond of just the flower girls."

Daisy hurried to join Glory, Persia, and Jade beside the pond.

The photographer bent over her

tripod and peered through her view-finder. She straightened up. "That's no good. One of you step to the front."

"I will!" Daisy started forward.

The alarm bell in her head clanged.

Daisy stopped herself. She backed up. "Jade's the shortest. She should be the one in front."

Daisy stood between Glory and Persia, behind Jade.

Glory and Persia hung their arms around Daisy's shoulders. They leaned in until their heads bumped hers. Jade leaned backward to rest against her.

Daisy felt as though she'd lived this moment before. Or as if she'd glimpsed it from another point of view . . .

"Girls, would you stop giggling?" said the photographer.

79

Glory gave the others a sharp nod.

In unison they all cried, "No!"

Click! The photographer snapped the picture.

There was roast beef at the reception and jerk chicken stew. There were black-eyed peas, Yorkshire pudding, and plantains—fried, roasted, and in chips.

The wedding cake was carrot with white icing. It was four tiers high. Standing at attention on the top tier were bride and groom dolls.

Dr. Adele and Grandaddy Lester sliced the bottom tier with a silver cake knife.

Click!

Grandaddy Lester held the slice to Dr. Adele's lips.

She took a ladylike bite.

Click!

Dr. Adele lifted a slice of the dark, moist cake to Grandaddy Lester's lips. She gave him her sweetest smile.

Grandaddy Lester leaned forward. He opened his mouth . . .

Dr. Adele pressed the cake in his face.

Relatives gasped.

Click!

"What a devil she is!" said one guest.

Another chuckled. "What a tease!"

Heather nudged Daisy. "Are you sure Dr. Adele's not your real grandmother? She acts just like you!"

While everyone held their breath and watched, Grandaddy Lester caught a surprised Dr. Adele by the shoulders. He pulled her to him and gave her a big, face-mashing kiss.

When he let her go, they turned to face the guests.

Butter icing and wedding cake crumbs plastered both their faces.

They both were laughing.

Daisy thought, *My real grandmother . . . could she be?*

Click!

"This is for you," said Glory.

"For singing with us," said Jade.

Persia held out a gift wrapped in gold paper and ivory ribbon. It was the size of an audiotape.

Daisy took it and opened it.

It *was* an audiotape.

"It's a recording of us singing every song we know," said Persia, "minus the rhythm part."

"Glory recorded the rhythm part separately after each song," said Jade.

Glory grinned at Daisy. "You can learn that part and then sing along with us on the tape."

Daisy lifted the tape from the box. She read the label: DAISY'S TAPE, WITH LOVE FROM THE GRANDDAUGHTERS. At each corner of the label was a picture. A fiery-rayed sun. A crescent moon. A cluster of stars. And . . . a daisy with a center of gold.

She looked up at the granddaughters. "You made this ahead of time. How did you know I'd sing my part the right way?"

"Simple," said Jade. "Last night, before we went to bed, we enchanted you."

Daisy stared from Jade to the others.

"That's right," said Glory.

Persia nodded.

Daisy remembered her bad dreams. She remembered making the decision . . .

Had *she* made the decision?

All three granddaughters burst out laughing.

"Just kidding," said Jade.

"No one enchanted you," said Glory.

Daisy tossed her head. "I knew that."

Still, as she turned over the tape in her hands, she couldn't help but wonder . . .

Click!

Waiters served the wedding cake.

The dance band played.

Daisy glanced around their "children's" table. On one side Rose and Glory faced one another and chatted intently about favorite books. On the other side Persia and Violet whispered about dolls. Jade and Heather had left their side-by-side places to study people's outfits.

"That lady's too old to wear ruffles," said Jade.

"That guy should get a better-fitting hairpiece," said Heather.

Daisy watched her friends.

None was paying attention to her.

But Daisy didn't feel as if she was losing them. She felt relaxed, warm, filled with something larger than she was. . . .

Click!

 86

Chapter 10

Three days later Daisy braked to a stop at Slow Creek Beach.

The granddaughters had left for home that morning. Daisy missed them already. Still . . .

There was something nice about having her life back to normal.

She parked her bike in a rack and headed down to the shore.

Rose, Violet, and Heather were already in the water.

Heather was saying, "If Glory, Persia, and Jade are Dr. Adele's granddaughters, where were their parents? Why weren't

Adele's sons and daughters at the wedding?"

"Persia told me it was too expensive for all of them to make the trip," said Violet.

"Glory told me their parents had to stay home with younger children," said Rose.

Daisy said, "They love their island and hate our 'cold' weather. That's what Jade told me."

Heather stood in waist-deep water. She held out her arms and let herself fall backward. "I wish I could see that island paradise."

Daisy waded into the creek. "The granddaughters invited me to visit. Next winter. Grandaddy and Dr. Adele—*Gran* Adele—are going. They offered to take me along. Mom and Dad said, 'Maybe . . . '"

"You are so lucky!" said Heather.

"Daisy's not lucky. She's special," said Violet.

Rose spouted an arc of water as if she were a fountain. "Daisy's the best!"

"Cut it out, you guys!" Daisy felt embarrassed. "It's the *granddaughters* who live on the island. They're the special ones." Saying so didn't make her feel nervous or jealous. It was nice knowing kids who were special in ways she wasn't. That was why she liked Rose, Violet, and Heather. Each was different from Daisy. Each was special in her own way.

"You never told us. . . . What made you decide to go along with the granddaughters' way of singing?" asked Rose.

"What changed your mind?" asked Violet.

Daisy scrambled back to the shore.

She rummaged in her backpack and pulled out a wedding photo.

The others left the water and gathered around her to look.

The photo showed Daisy singing with the granddaughters at the reception. But instead of standing on the floor, all four girls appeared to be floating in space. Instead of looking solid, their bodies appeared transparent and filled with people, furniture, chandeliers, the wedding cake . . .

"It's a double exposure," said Heather. "Cool!"

Daisy gazed at the photo. "When we sang, I lost gravity. It felt exactly like this picture."

"Wowww!" Everyone gazed at the photo.

"So that's why you sang your part that way," said Heather.

"It felt better to lose gravity than to stand out," said Violet.

Rose said, "Once you'd gotten that feeling, you had to change your plan, right?"

"I guess so. . . ." Daisy thought back to the wedding and her moment of decision. There was still something that bothered her. Something the granddaughters had said at the reception . . .

Daisy looked from Heather to Violet to Rose. She hesitated. "Do you believe in enchantment?"

"*Magical* enchantment . . . ?" Violet sang the words.

"*Magical* enchantment . . . ?" Heather sang them on a higher note.

Rose sang them on a note that was

higher still. "*Magical* enchantment . . . ?"

All three girls held their notes.

Daisy's insides shimmered and tingled.

Pleasure swelled in her chest.

Magical enchantment . . . ? Daisy didn't know whether she believed in it or not. She didn't care. All Daisy cared about was finding her note and joining in.